T0245902

DARK MAN

THE PAST IS DARK

by Peter Lancett

illustrated by Jan Pedroietta

SADDLEBACK
EDUCATIONAL PUBLISHING

DARK MAN

Blue Series

The Dark Fire of Doom
Destiny in the Dark
The Face in the Dark Mirror

The Dark Never Hides
Escape from the Dark
Fear in the Dark

Orange Series

Danger in the Dark
The Dark Dreams
The Dark Glass

The Dark Side of Magic
The Dark Waters of Time
The Shadow in the Dark

Green Series

The Dark Candle
The Dark Machine
The Dark Words

The Day is Dark
Dying for the Dark
Killer in the Dark

Yellow Series

The Bridge of Dark Tears
The Dark Garden
The Dark Music

The Dark River
The Past is Dark
Playing the Dark Game

© Ransom Publishing Ltd. 2011

Text © Peter Lancett 2011

Illustrations © Jan Pedroietta 2011

David Strachan, The Old Man and The Shadow Masters appear
by kind permission of Peter Lancett

This edition is published by arrangement with Ransom Publishing Ltd.

SADDLEBACK
EDUCATIONAL PUBLISHING
www.sdlback.com

© 2012 by Saddleback Educational Publishing
All rights reserved. No part of this book may be reproduced in any form or by any means,
electronic or mechanical, including photocopying, recording, scanning, or by any information
storage and retrieval system, without the written permission of the publisher. SADDLEBACK
EDUCATIONAL PUBLISHING and any associated logos are trademarks and/or registered
trademarks of Saddleback Educational Publishing.

ISBN-13: 978-1-61651-295-8
ISBN-10: 1-61651-295-4

Printed in U.S.A.

20 19 18 17 16   4 5 6 7 8

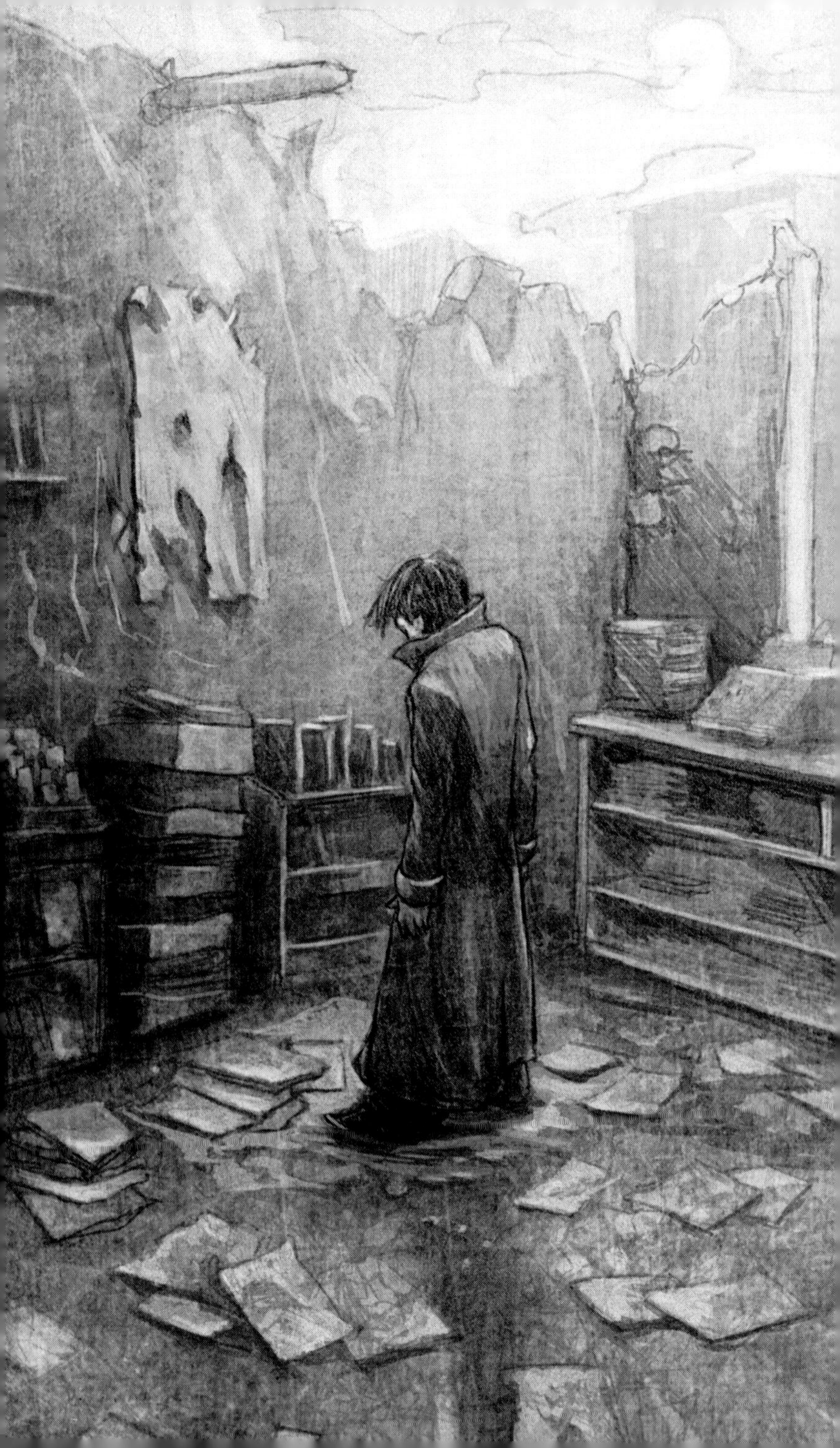

Chapter One:
In the Empty Store

The Dark Man stands in a ruined store.

Moonlight streams in where there was once a roof.

The Dark Man is here because he has been told that a Shadow Master was here earlier.

But the store is empty.

Old magazines are scattered around.

The Dark Man knows little about his past,
only that he was once called David.

To the Dark Man, the past is dark.

All he knows is that he must help the Old Man to stop the Shadow Masters.

The Shadow Masters want to ruin the whole city.

When the whole city is rotten, they will make slaves of the people.

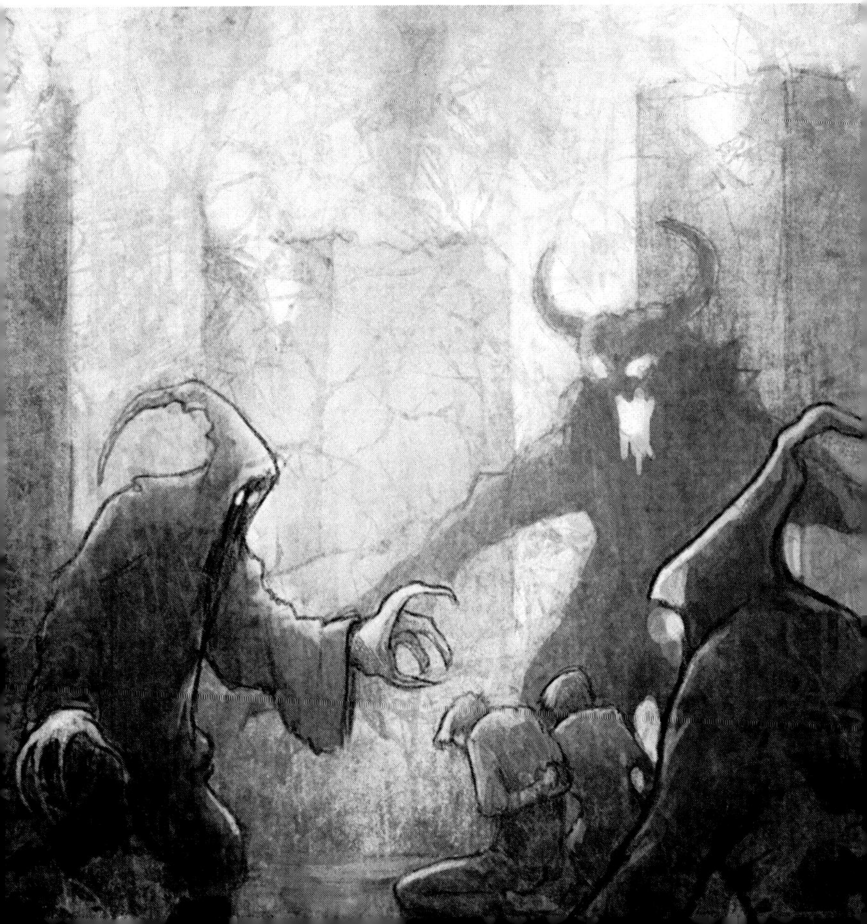

The Dark Man thinks hard, trying to remember the time before the Shadow Masters.

The memories do not come.

The glossy cover of a magazine shines in the moonlight.

The Dark Man stoops to pick it up.

On the cover there is a photograph of a large boat.

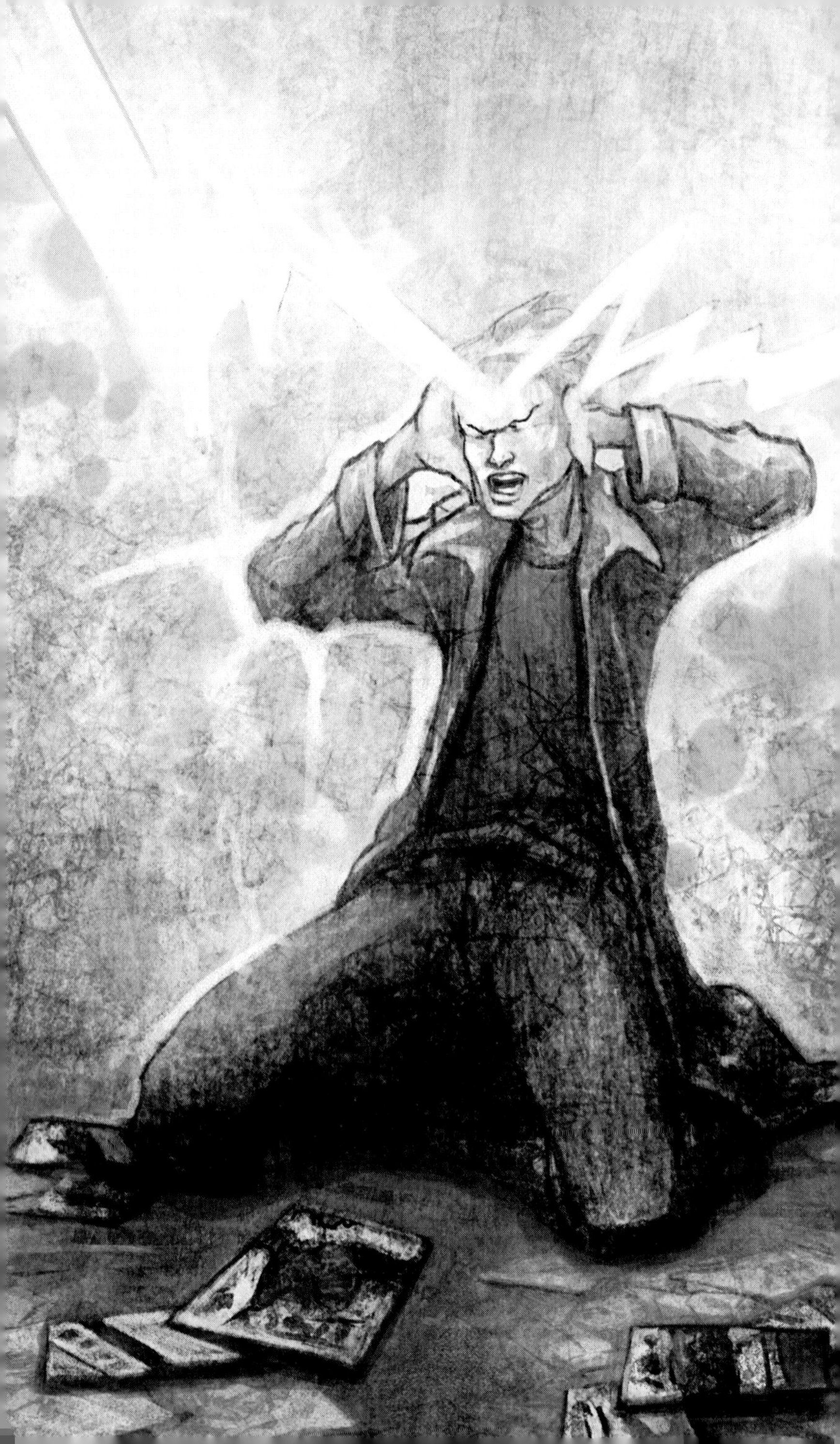

A sharp pain shoots through the Dark Man's head.

He drops the magazine and puts his hands over his ears, as he falls to his knees.

Chapter Two:
Where the Forest Ends

There is a flash of white light, and when the Dark Man opens his eyes, he is no longer in the ruined store.

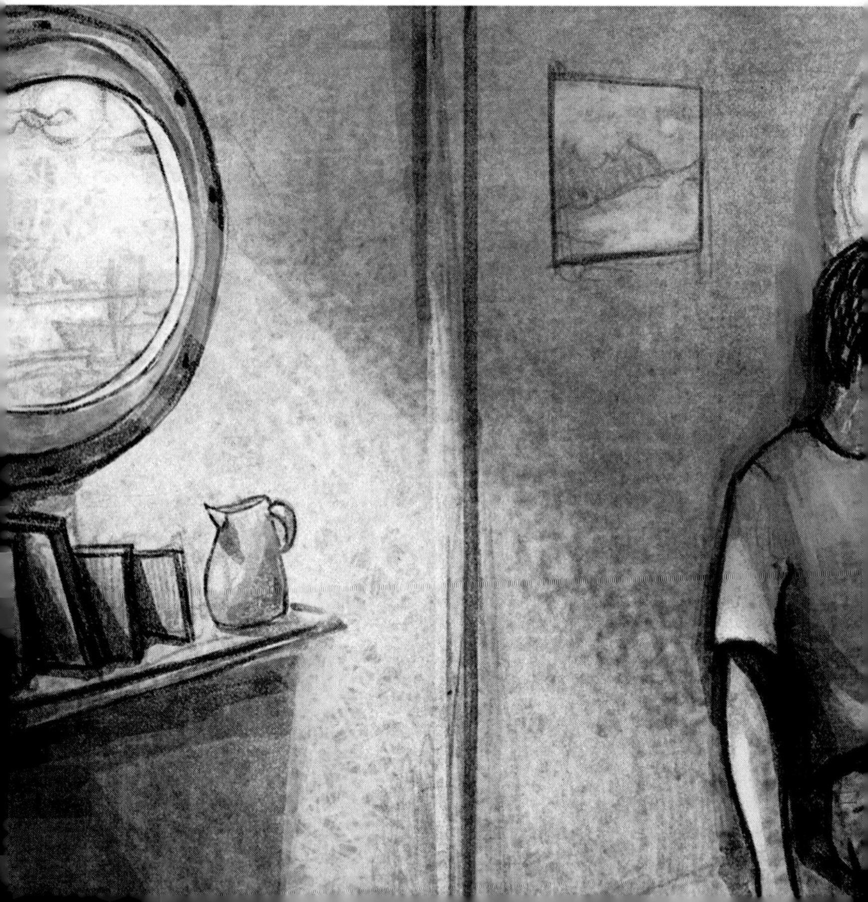

He is sitting in the cabin of a large boat in a sunny harbor.

Sitting opposite is a beautiful, blonde girl.

He knows that her name is Astrid, and that she is his girlfriend.

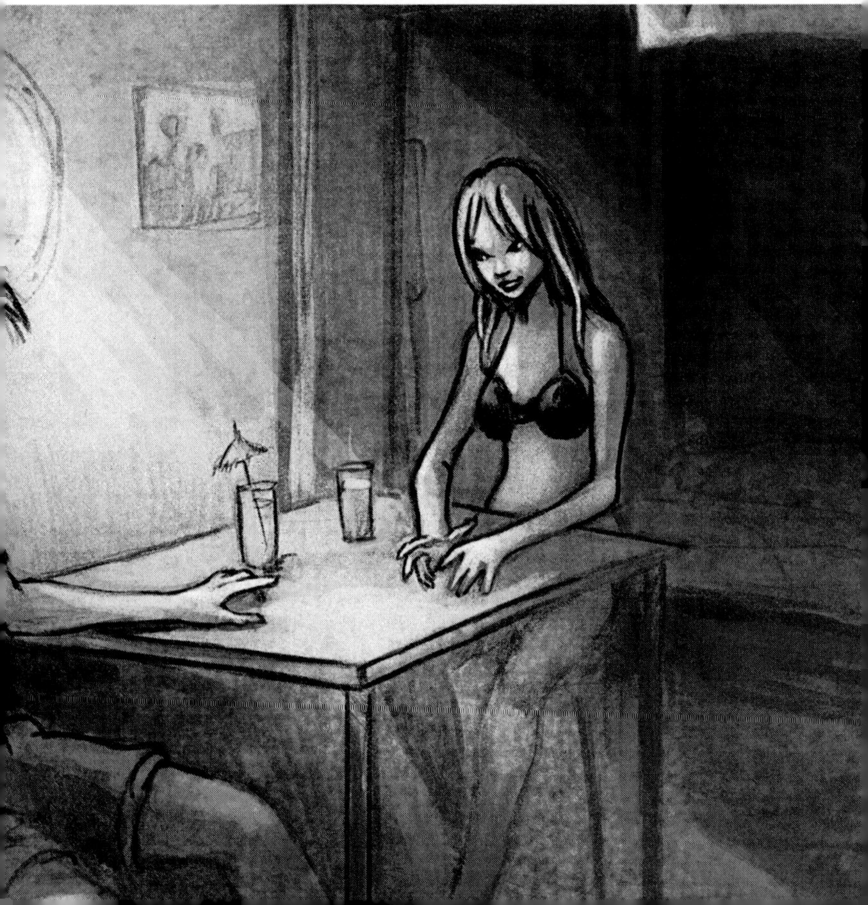

"David, can we go up to the big house tonight, the one hidden in the forest?" Astrid asks.

"Why do you want to go?" the Dark Man replies.

"It looks spooky. I want to see what it looks like in the dark. We can sneak over the wall, and look at it from the trees," Astrid says.

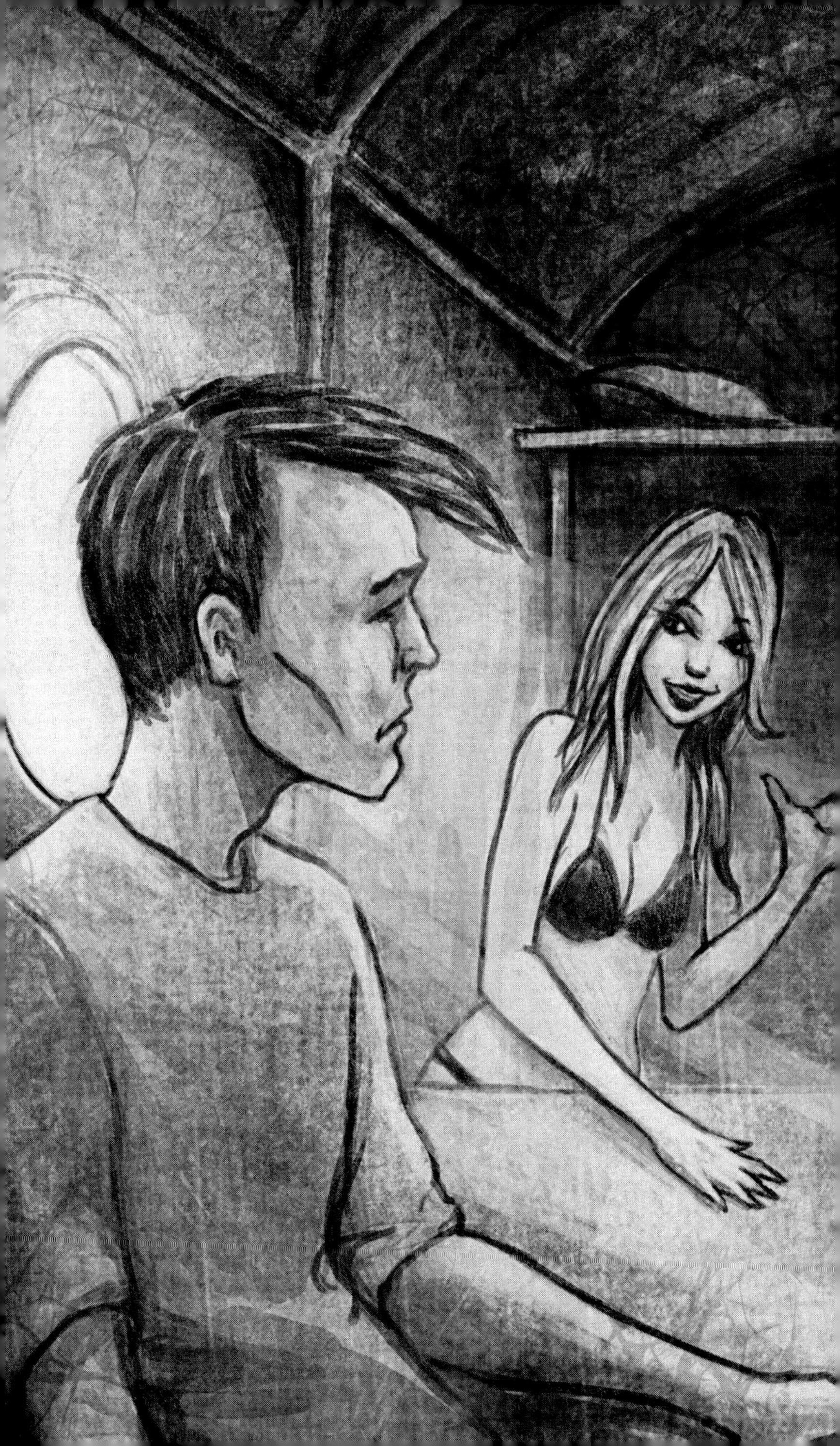

A memory comes to the Dark Man.

He was once a soldier.

He knows how to sneak through the forest.

"Yes," he says. "If you really want to. We can go tonight."

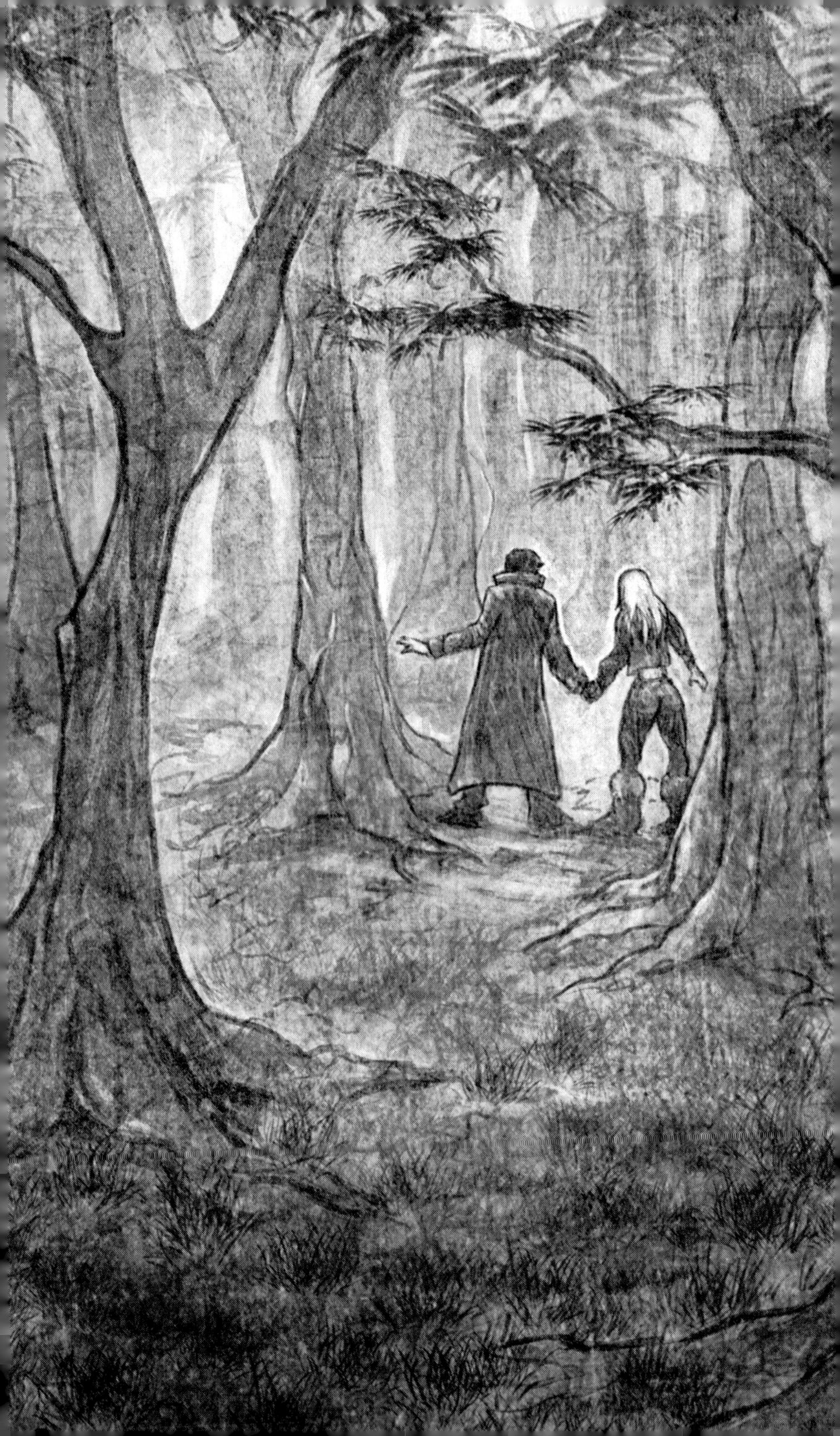

The Dark Man and Astrid creep between the trees in the forest.

They move slowly, making no noise.

The Dark Man shows Astrid how to tread with care.

"How long before we reach the house?" Astrid asks.

"Hush," the Dark Man whispers. "We must stay quiet. We are nearly there."

Soon, they come to where the forest ends.

Beyond the trees is a huge lawn.

Beyond the lawn is the house.

It is old and large with towers and high windows.

The windows are all dark.

"It looks like Dracula's castle," Astrid says.

Again, the Dark Man tells her to hush.

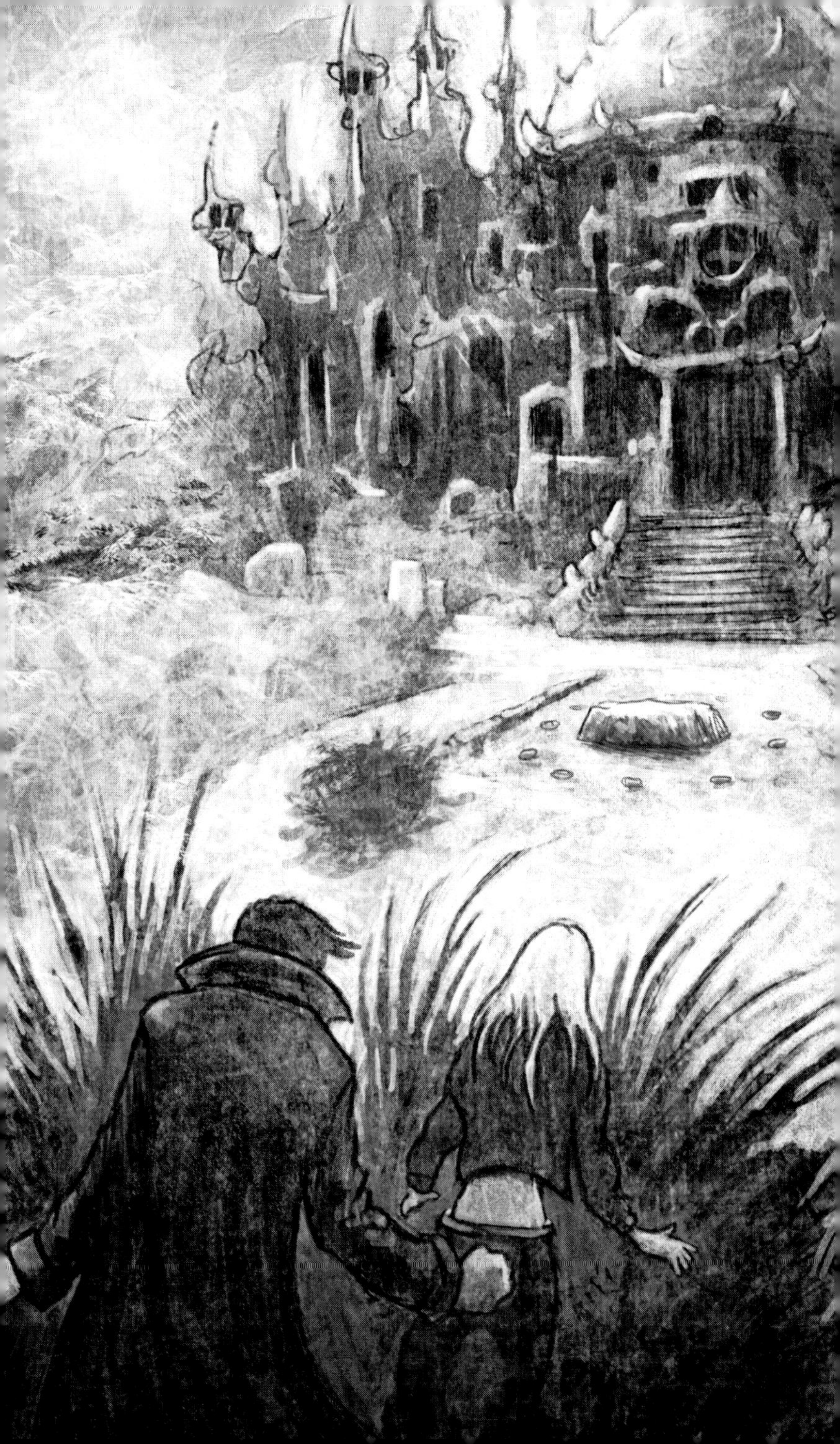

Chapter Three:
The White Stone

In the middle of the lawn there is a large, stone block.

"That stone looks like an altar," Astrid whispers.

Before the Dark Man can reply, the huge doors at the front of the house swing open.

The Dark Man and Astrid watch as hooded figures emerge from the doors.

Each hooded figure holds a candle.

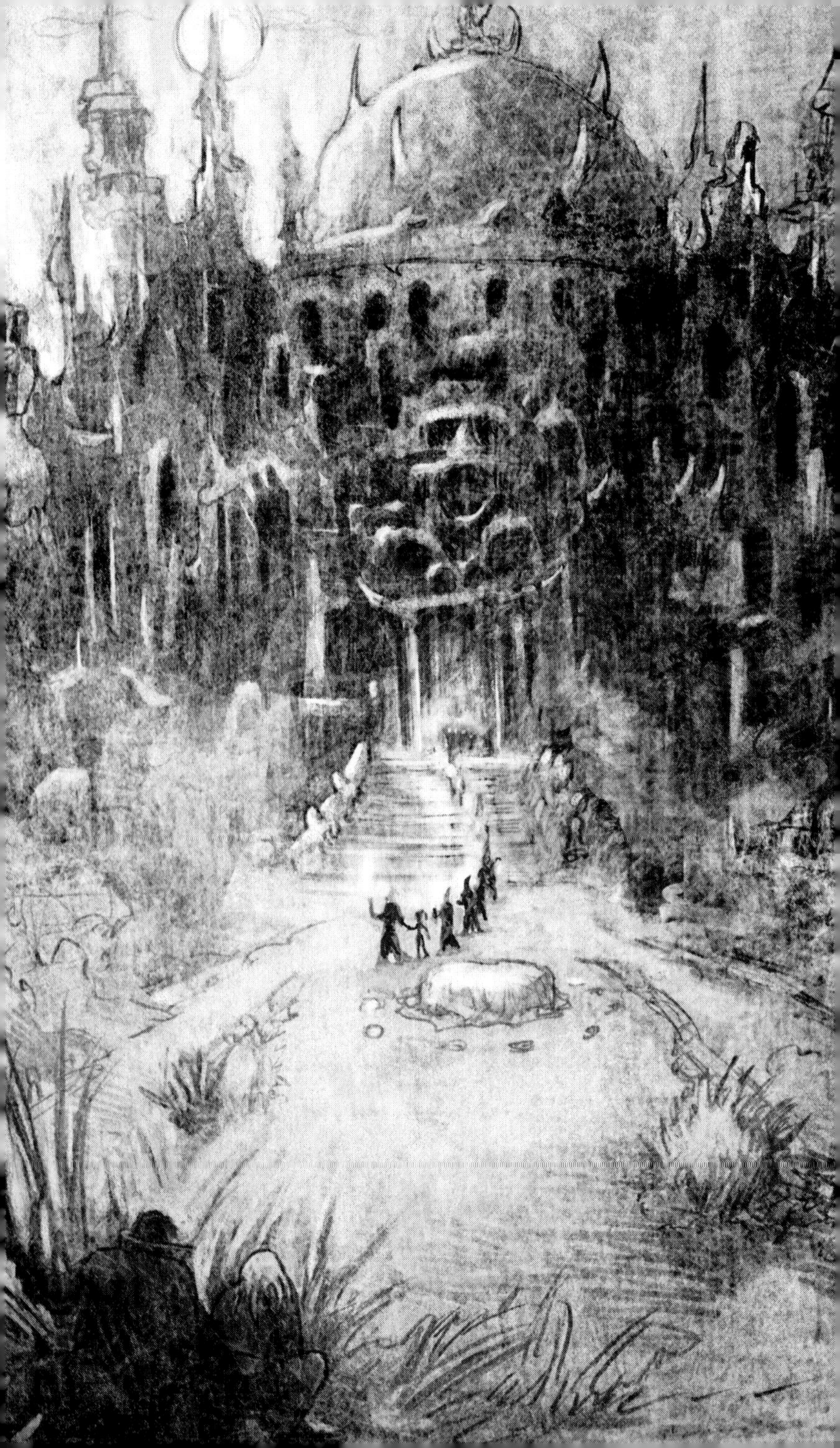

They form a line and walk slowly toward the center of the lawn.

The hooded figure at the front of the line is holding the hand of a little girl.

The Dark Man feels Astrid grab his hand.

She is holding tight.

He looks at her and sees that she is afraid.

"Shadow Masters," the Dark Man whispers, looking back to the hooded figures.

The Dark Man and Astrid watch as the Shadow Masters form a circle around the white stone block on the lawn.

The little girl is lifted up to stand upon the stone block.

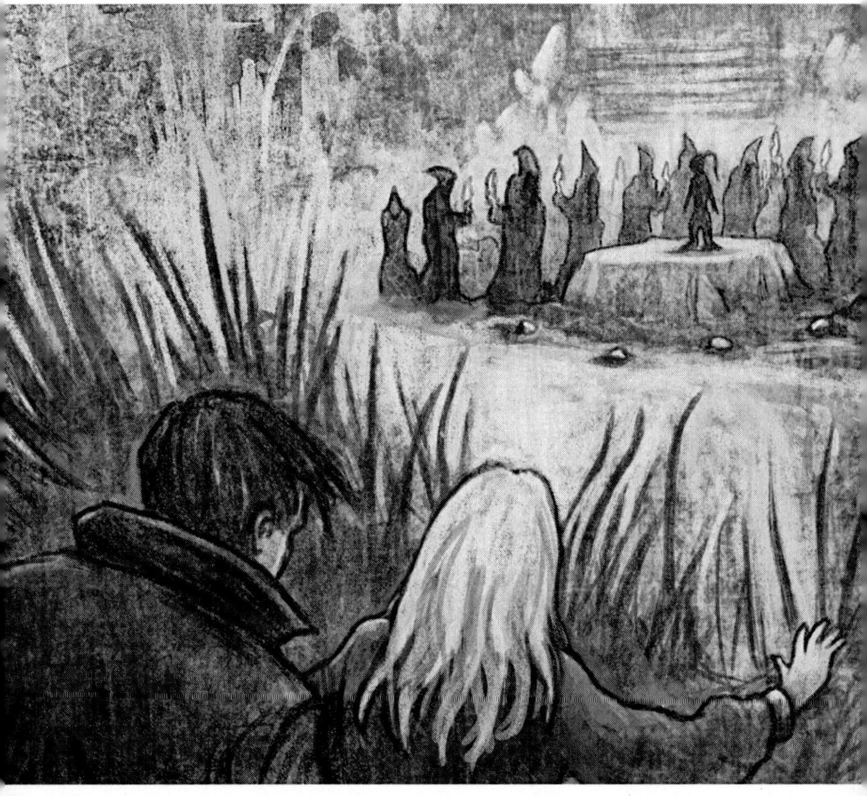

A Shadow Master points a silver wand and yellow flames start to burn at the corners of the white stone.

Then the Shadow Master dances around the stone, chanting secret words.

There is a flash of blue light, and suddenly a small demon is standing on the stone, next to the little girl.

The little girl is sobbing.

Astrid can stand it no longer.

"No!" she screams, getting to her feet.

The Shadow Masters all turn and silently start running toward them.

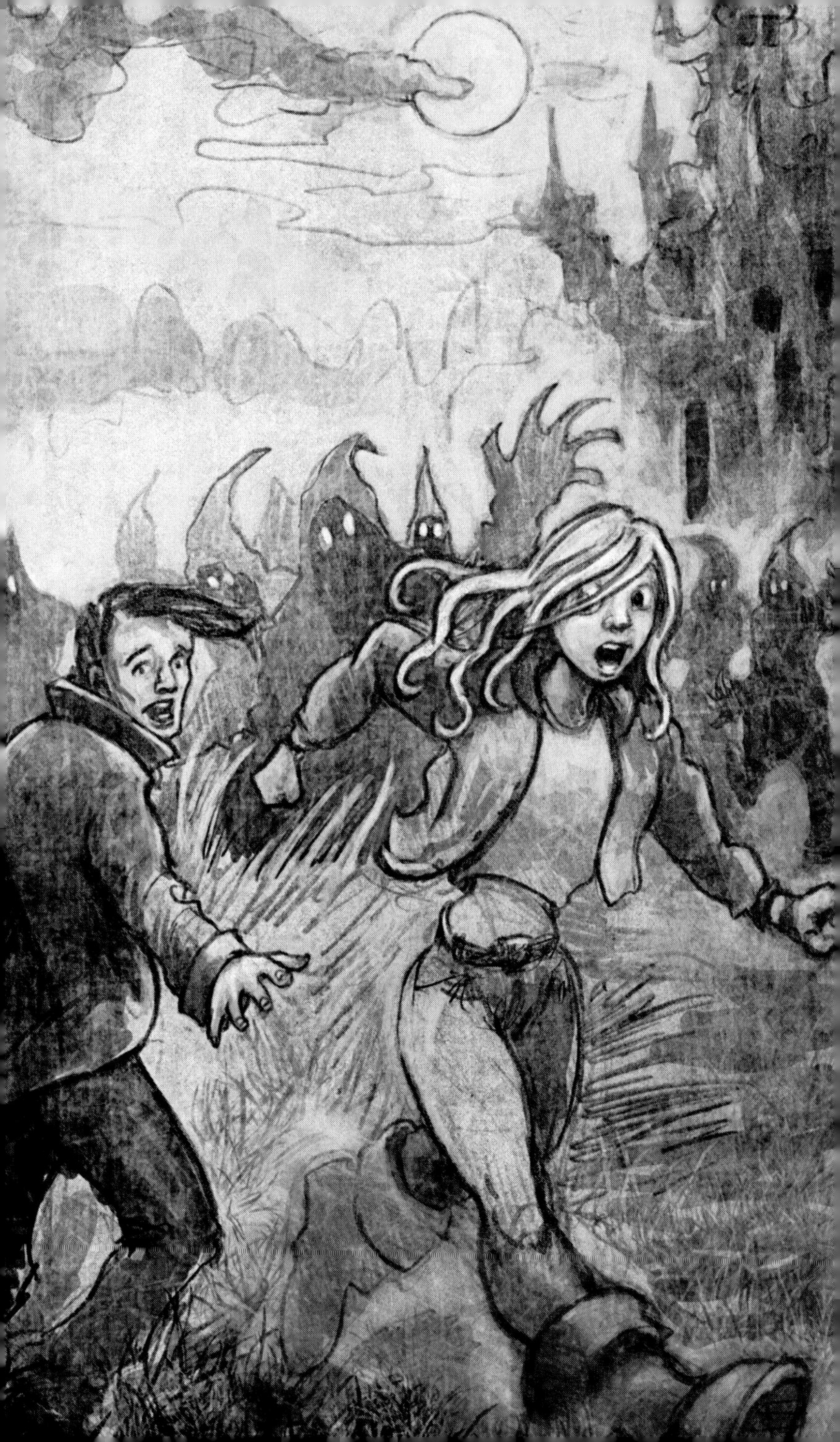

"Come on! We've got to get out of here," the Dark Man hisses.

He takes Astrid's hand, and they run through the forest, no longer caring about the noise they are making.

They keep running, even when they can no longer hear sounds of the Shadow Masters chasing them.

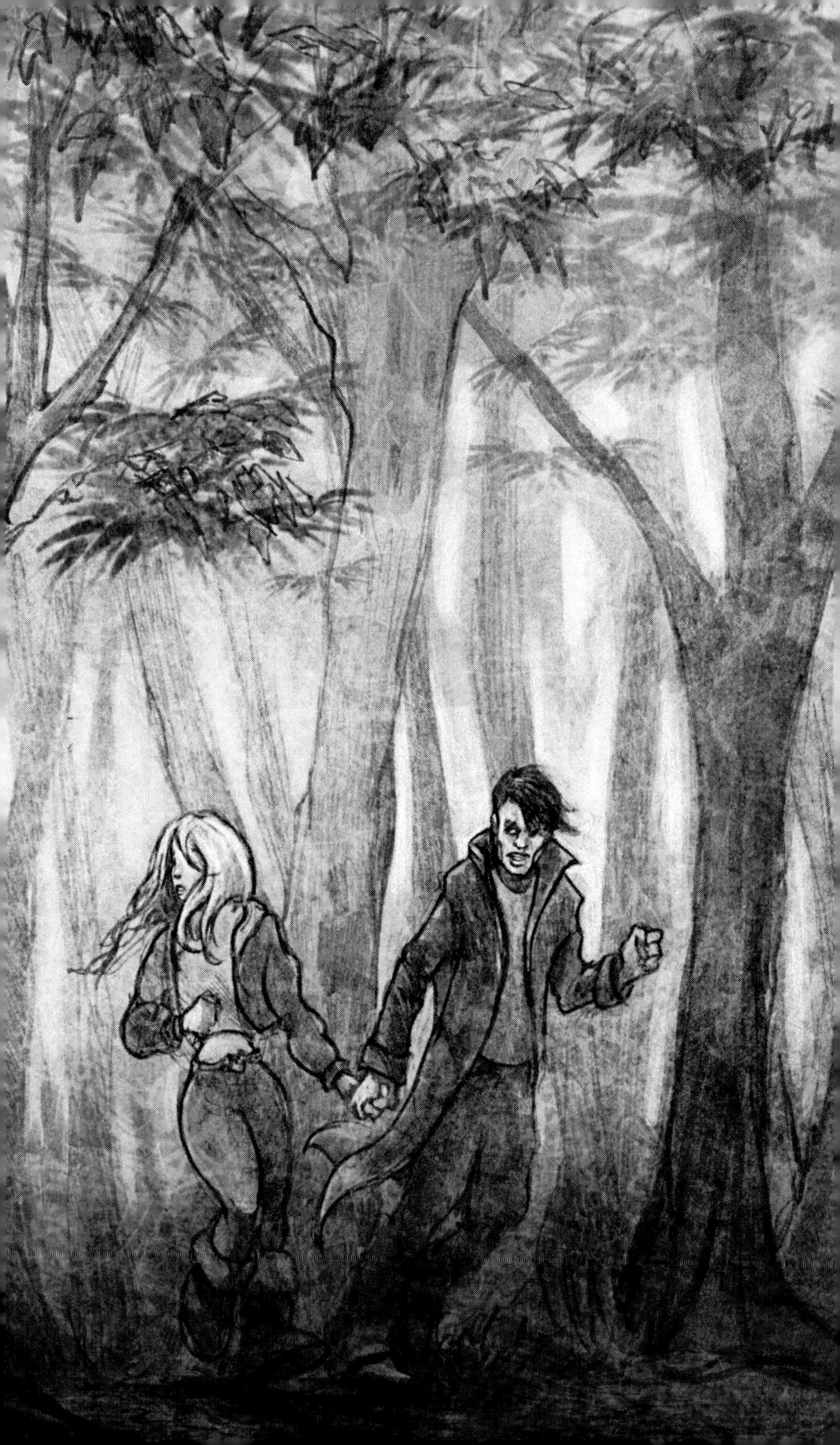

Chapter Four:
A Vision of the Past

Suddenly, a slender figure steps out from behind a tree in front of them.

It is a man, very thin, like a skeleton.

His face has been burned and the skin stretches tight, so that he looks like a grinning skull.

The Dark Man dives to one side, but Astrid just stops and stands rigid with fear.

The thin man lifts a blowpipe to his lips.

"Astrid, get down!" the Dark Man shouts.

But she is too scared to move.

A dart from the blowpipe hits her neck, and she drops to the ground.

The dart must be drugged.

Before the Dark Man can move, more figures appear from behind trees to carry Astrid away.

Then the thin man turns toward the Dark Man and lifts the blowpipe to his lips again.

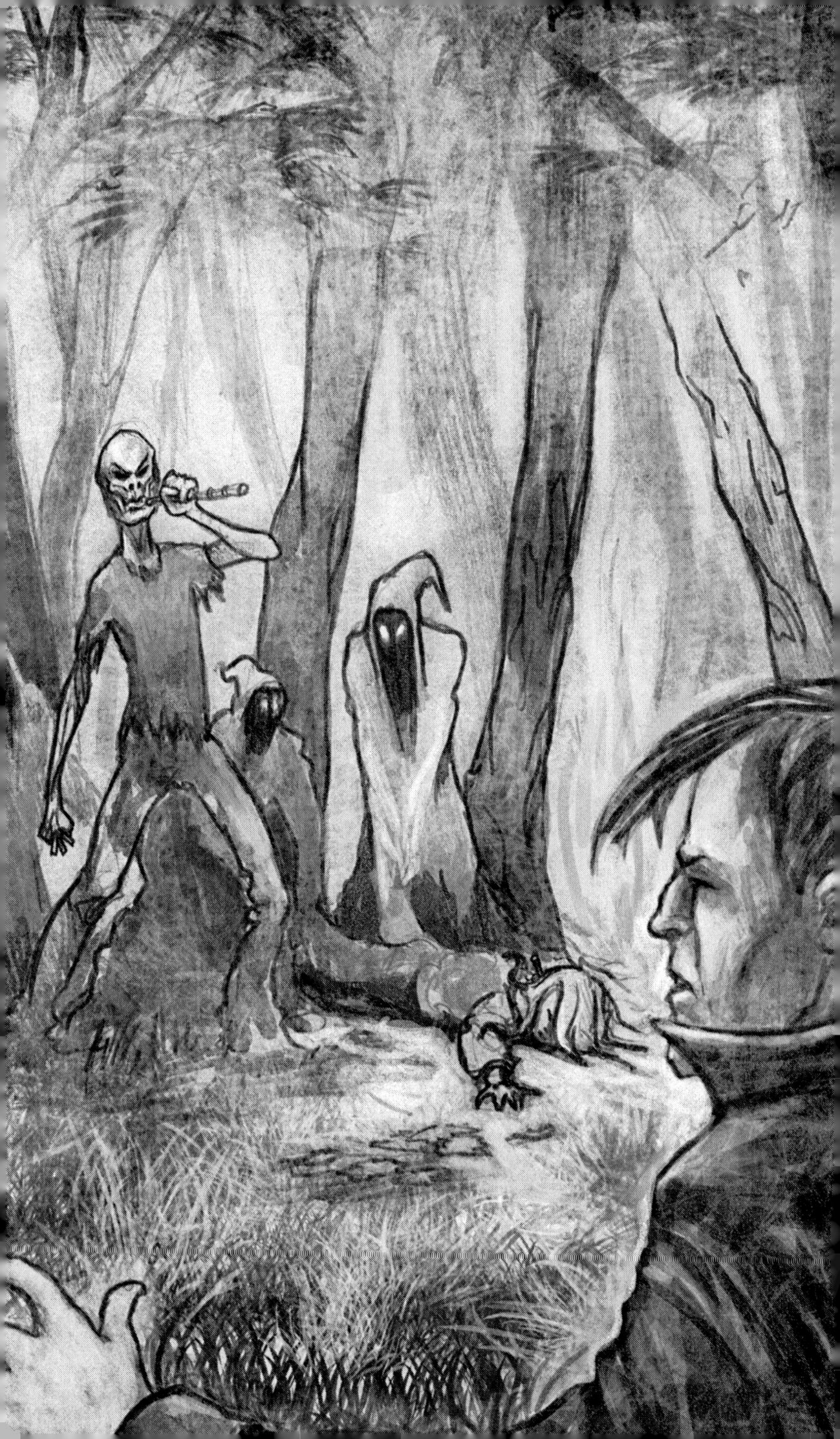

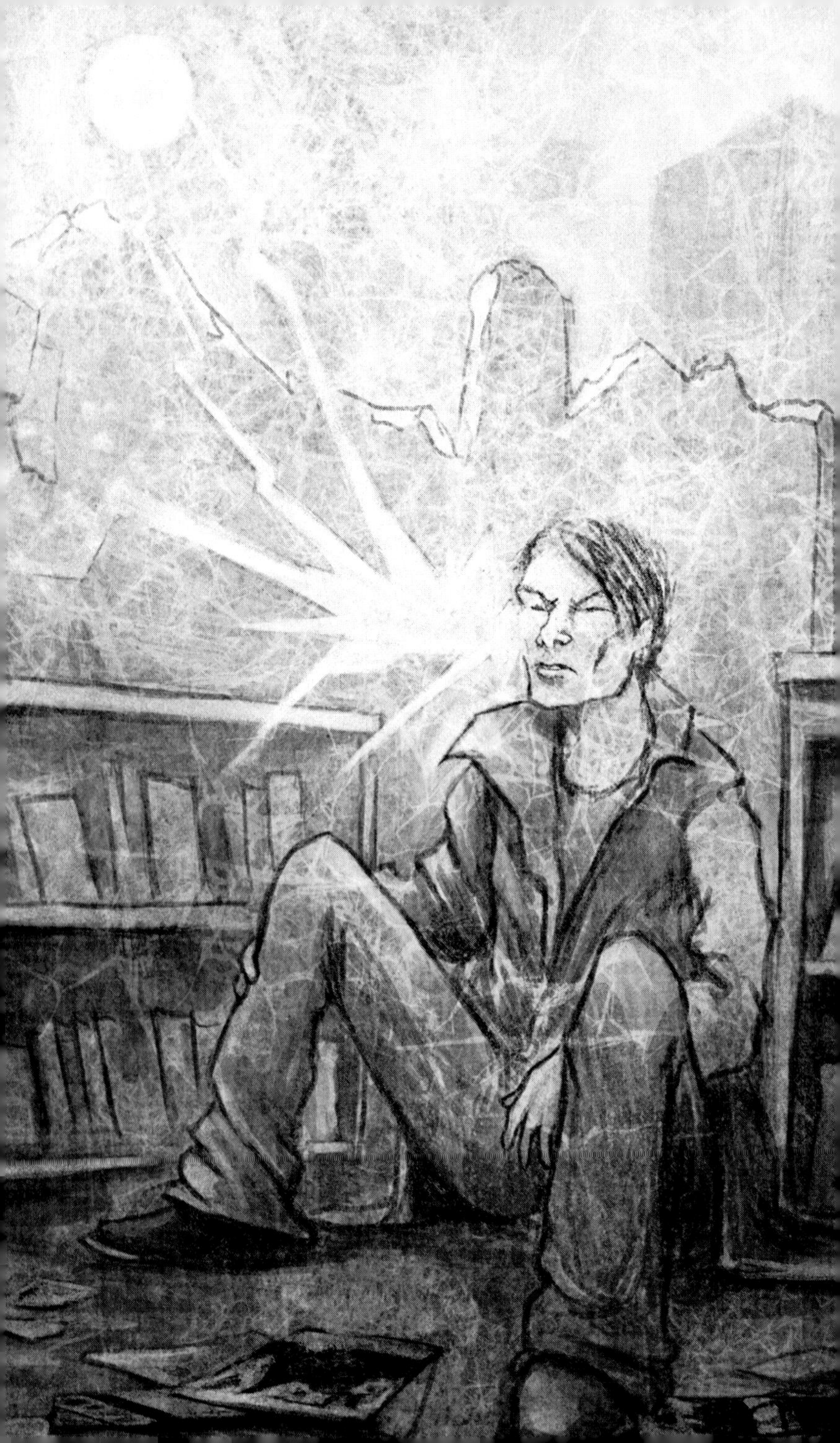

There is another flash of white light, and when the Dark Man opens his eyes, he is sitting on the floor of the ruined store.

It is no longer night, and the sun shines through the ruined roof.

He knows that his mind has given him a vision of the past.

He has been shown how the Shadow Masters took Astrid from him, long, long ago.

In his sadness, he buries his face in his hands.

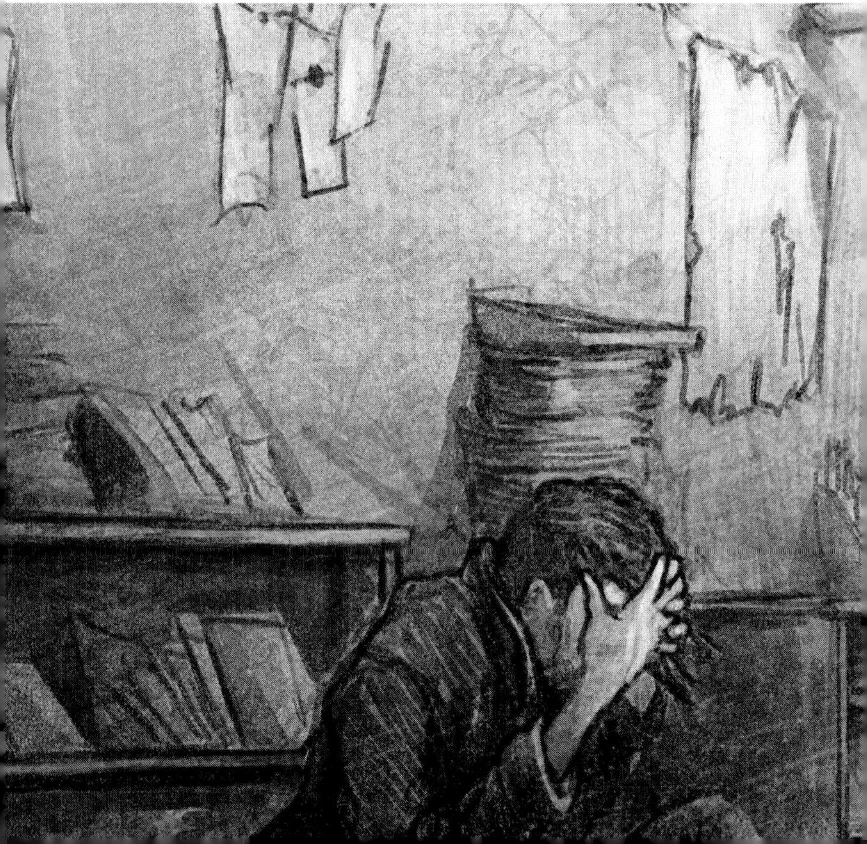

"Come, stand up," a voice says gently, after a few moments have passed.

The Dark Man looks up.

The Old Man is standing before him.

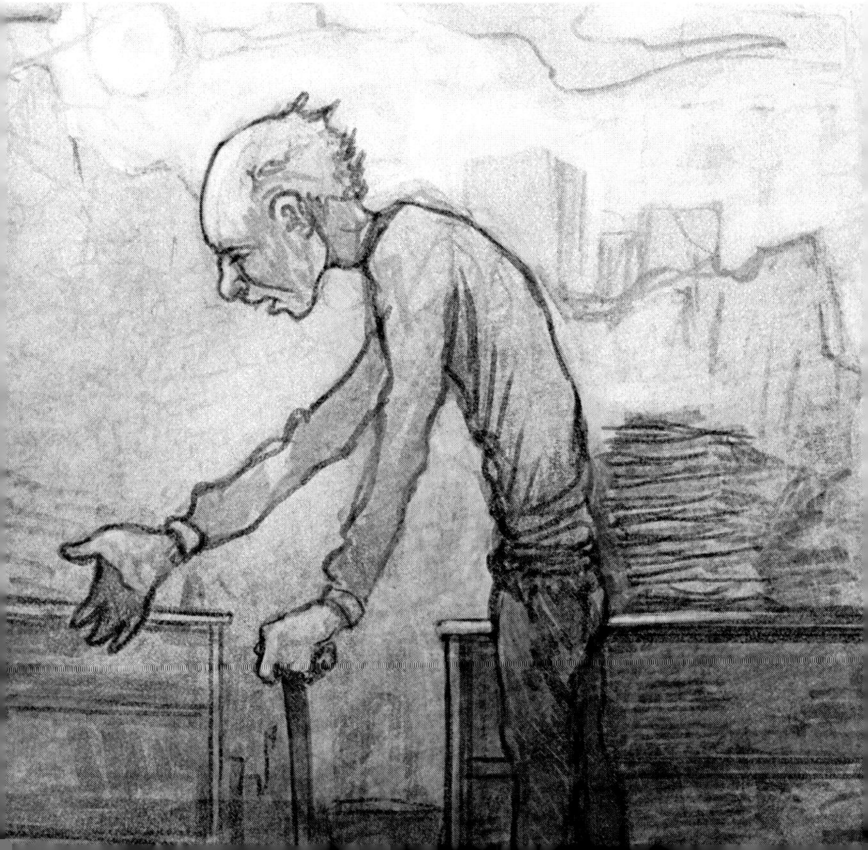

"You have remembered something from the past," the Old Man says, as the Dark Man rises from the dusty floor.

The Dark Man nods, slowly.

"Remembering can be painful," the Old Man says.

The Dark Man nods in agreement once more.

He says nothing.

But he knows that the memory of Astrid will stay with him forever.

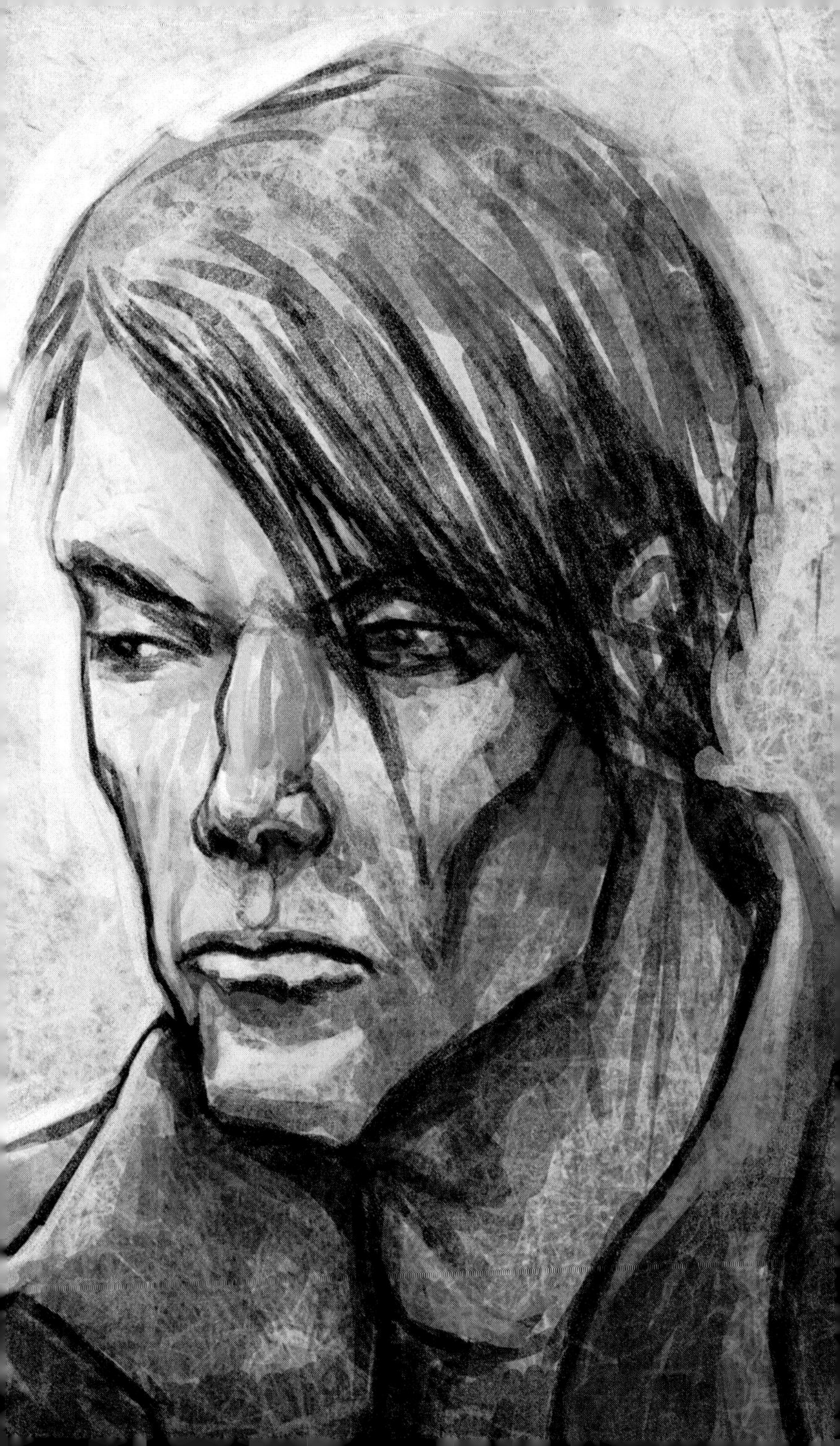

THE AUTHOR

Peter Lancett is a writer, editor, and filmmaker.
He has written many books and has just made
a feature film, *The Xlitherman*.

Peter now lives in New Zealand and California.